Enchantimals™

JOURNEY TO
FROZENWOOD

ORCHARD BOOKS
Carmelite House
50 Victoria Embankment
London EC4Y 0DZ

First published in the United Kingdom in 2019 by Orchard Books

A CIP catalogue record for this book is available
from the British Library.

ISBN 978 1 40835 649 4

1 3 5 7 9 10 8 6 4 2

Printed in Great Britain

Orchard Books
An imprint of Hachette Children's Group
Part of The Watts Publishing Group Limited
An Hachette UK Company
www.hachette.co.uk

www.hachettechildrens.co.uk

CHAPTER ONE
HEAT WAVE

Summertime was hot in Wonderwood.
The sun beat down through the
leaves. The flowers were wilting. Flick's
bushy red tail was drooping. Twist's
bunny ears hung low around her face.
Danessa was fanning Sprint with her
hands to help her bestie cool off. The
friends were all queuing for an ice cream

cone. Cool, delicious, refreshing ice cream from Preena's igloo truck – that was just the thing for a heat wave!

"You must be so hot in your fur coat," Danessa said to her bestie.

Sprint stamped his hoof in agreement. He was. All the animals were hot. Too hot! Except Flap the peacock. He turned his face towards the sun and beamed happily. He was warm at last. Finally, Wonderwood was more like a jungle.

"Which flavour are you getting?" Danessa asked Sage.

"Caper and I like all kinds of berry ice creams," answered Sage. "Blueberry, strawberry—"

Caper the skunk blew through her lips.

"And raspberry!" Sage added with a giggle.

With the tip of her tail, Flick wiped away a bead of perspiration from Felicity's brow.

"I'll be happy with any flavour just as long as it's cold!" said Felicity.

Bree and Twist hopped forwards in the queue. "We'll have two cones of carrot cake," Bree told Preena and her penguin bestie, Jayla. Mmm! She couldn't wait. It was going to taste so good.

Flap waved his long feathers happily. He and Patter were getting tutti-frutti!

Danessa ordered pistachio for herself and Sprint. Pistachio ice cream was green just like the tall grass they loved to run through. Danessa took the two cones from Preena and pranced over to a picnic table. Ice cream was just what they all needed.

But before she could take one lick, the cool scoop of pistachio had turned into a sticky green mess dripping over her hand.

"Oh no!" Danessa cried. "We're all sticky! Don't you worry, Sprint. I've got some tissues to clean off your hooves."

Twist held up her paws. They were covered in melted ice cream, too!

Danessa handed the bunny another tissue. What a mess!

Caper was frowning. Blobs of raspberry ice cream were dripping out of the bottom of her cone.

"It's too hot even for ice cream!" exclaimed Felicity.

The sun was melting the ice cream as soon as it was scooped.

Even Flap was disappointed. His claws were covered in melted tutti-frutti.

He liked warm weather but not warm ice cream goop. He threw his cone in the bin.

"We'll just have to find another way to cool off," said Danessa. "I know! Maybe we should talk about cool things ... like snowmen."

Flick pulled out her sketch pad and began drawing a wintertime scene with evergreen trees and snowflakes.

"And icicles!" suggested Sage, looking over her shoulder.

"And ice-skating and sledging and hot chocolate by the fire ..." Bree gushed. "Oops! Now I'm feeling hot again."

Fanci Flamingo stepped past the girls, shaking her head. "Whatever am I going to do?" She sighed, looking down at the melted ice cream cone in her hands. "This is just terrible! Terrible!"

"It's just ice cream," Danessa said, trying to comfort her.

"Mostly just cream at this point," joked Sage, looking down at her sticky hands. A big droplet of melted ice cream dripped onto Flick's sketch pad.

"My garden party is ruined," Fanci cried, upset. "I promised on the invitation that I would be serving ice cream."

"You did!" remembered Bree. "Everyone's been talking about how much fun it is going to be."

"But it won't be any fun if all the ice cream melts!" wailed Fanci. She held up the empty cone in her sticky hands.

"There, there," said Danessa, patting her gently on the shoulder. "This isn't a problem at all. We can solve this, can't we, girls?" Beside her, Sprint, her bestie, nodded his antlers.

Sage and Bree exchanged a glance. Could they? How?

"Don't fret," Danessa told Fanci. "We'll find some ice cream that doesn't melt for your party! How about that?"

Fanci's face brightened. "Really?"

Felicity smiled nervously. Patter gulped. Sage watched more customers walk away from Preena's ice cream truck, staring at the melted messes in their hands.

Danessa patted her friend on the shoulder again reassuringly. "You've been so sweet to invite everyone to your garden party. Don't you worry about the ice cream. We'll take care of that. That's what friends do for one another!"

Sprint smiled and stamped his hoof

in agreement. The other girls nodded.
Danessa was right, they needed to
try to help Fanci! But where in
Wonderwood could they find ice
cream that didn't melt?

CHAPTER TWO
AN ICE-COLD IDEA

The air was a little cooler near Babbling
Brook. The girls and their besties sat
down in the shade to cool off. What was
Danessa's plan? Where were they ever
going to find ice cream that didn't melt?

Felicity's brow wrinkled as she
thought. "I've travelled to a lot of exciting
places. But I've never ever heard of ice
cream that doesn't melt."

"We didn't have it in Junglewood," Patter agreed. "We didn't have anything cold there."

Danessa was fanning herself with her straw hat. She noticed a hot, tired frog slowly hopping towards the brook. She reached out and gave it a helping hand. Ahh! It sighed and smiled as it plopped beneath the water. That was better.

"I don't know," admitted Danessa. "But I know that Fanci is counting on us. She needs our help. She really, really does. Really. We can save Fanci's garden party, right?"

Bree's pink ears were twitching with excitement. She couldn't resist a challenge. "How hard can it be? I just need to make a machine that combines the ingredients in a special new way so they turn too cold to melt. I'd need to hook up a mixing bowl to the ice maker on the refrigerator ..."

Twist began hopping up and down and waving her paws. She had so many ideas. Bree pulled out a notebook and began scribbling some of them down.

"We'll find some way to help, too," offered Sage. Caper nodded eagerly. "We know a lot about throwing a great party, don't we, Caper?"

Danessa clapped her hands. "See? I knew we could do it!"

"I think we should also talk to Preena," Felicity suggested. "If anyone knows about ice cream, it's her and Jayla."

"That's a great idea!" said Patter. "Maybe she knows a secret recipe."

"And we can go on a journey to find it!" exclaimed Felicity.

Flick wagged her ears happily and Felicity joined in. All of a sudden, this didn't seem like a problem; it seemed like an adventure.

"That is another great idea!" exclaimed Danessa. "Just because we've never heard of ice cream that doesn't melt, it doesn't mean it doesn't already exist. We should go and talk to Preena straight away."

"I'll stay here and work on my special never-melting ice cream machine," Bree offered.

"We can stay and help, too!" added Sage.

"That's an excellent idea!" Danessa agreed, smiling. Her friends were the best!

Sprint lowered his head so a little bird on the ground could climb onto his antlers. When he stood up, Danessa reached over and put the little bird back into its nest. "It's always better to have lots of different ways to solve a problem, isn't it, Sprint?"

Danessa was relieved. Her friends were so resourceful. They were going to save Fanci's party!

The most surprising thing was that no one even noticed the heat anymore. They were too excited about their project!

CHAPTER THREE
THE HEAT IS ON!

The sun was still beating down hotter than ever. But no more customers were standing in front of the igloo truck. Jayla started waving her flippers when she saw the girls approaching.

"What would you like, Felicity? Another cone of tutti-frutti for you, Patter?" Preena asked hopefully.

"Ummm, is there a flavour that doesn't melt?" asked Patter.

"You know, like a special never-melting flavour?" Felicity added.

"We promised Fanci we'd get her some for her garden party," explained Danessa.

"Never-melting ice cream?" Preena scratched her head. "I've never heard of it. In Frozenwood we have lots of different flavours. Not just chocolate and vanilla but watermelon and seaweed and corn on the cob—"

"Corn on the cob?!" interrupted Danessa. "That sounds delicious!"

"Mmmmmm," agreed Sprint. He loved corn, too. All deer did.

"Someday you'll have to travel to Frozenwood and try some," Preena told Danessa.

"So you've never heard of ice cream

that doesn't melt?" Patter asked Preena.

Jayla and Preena exchanged a glance.
"There's a legend about a time when
there was too much ice cream," Preena
began.

"How can you have too much ice
cream?" Felicity giggled.

"Once upon a time, it started snowing
ice cream," said Preena. "There was ice
cream for breakfast and ice cream for
lunch and ice cream for dinner. There
was ice cream piling up over the houses.
But that's just a legend. That's the story I
heard when I was little."

"Still, it sounds wonderful!" said
Felicity, her eyes wide. "I would love to
see that."

"I would love to taste that!" Patter
added.

"Brrrrrr." Flap shivered. It sounded cold to the peacock. Very cold.

Jayla nodded. "Brrr," the penguin repeated. Except she liked being cold. At least the igloo truck was air-conditioned!

"There's another story I heard, about how once in Frozenwood there wasn't any ice cream at all," continued Preena.

"Did it get too hot? Like here?" asked Danessa.

"No." Preena shook her head. "They ran out of cream and had to make ice milk!" She giggled.

"Does ice milk melt?" asked Patter.

"Even faster than ice cream," Preena answered. "Or at least it did in the story."

Danessa was beginning to feel worried. At least Bree was working on a new invention. Maybe she would solve the problem of never-melting ice cream. Oh deer! She had promised Fanci she would help, but what if she couldn't?

Seeing her friends around the ice cream truck, Sage came over with her bestie, Caper, to see what was happening – and to order a cone of honey ice cream.

"It's going to melt really fast," Preena reminded her as she scooped the cone.

"That's okay." Sage laughed. "We don't mind if we get sticky, do we, Caper?"

Caper took her cone from Preena and began licking it as fast as she could.

"Brain freeze!" Sage exclaimed as she tried to gobble up her ice cream before it turned to liquid. But it just wasn't possible. She licked the melted ice cream off her hands. "It still tastes like honey," she said happily.

"Mmmmmm," murmured Caper.

"But look at my T-shirt!" exclaimed Sage. It was covered in splotches of melted honey ice cream. "Oh, that's no good at all. I'll have to go and change."

Patter's eyes widened. "That's why we have to find never-melting ice cream! Can you imagine if everyone's garden party clothes were ruined?"

"Are you sure you've never heard any stories about never-melting ice cream?" Danessa asked.

Preena and Jayla shook their heads sadly.

"There isn't a folk tale or a legend about ice cream that's always frozen?" urged Felicity.

Jayla's blue eyes widened. A grin

spread across Preena's face. "Why didn't you say so in the first place?"

"What? What?" asked all the girls together. What had Felicity said?

"I've never heard of never-melting ice cream," Preena explained, "but everyone in Frozenwood knows the legend of the always-frozen ice cream."

"Oh!" all the girls gasped.

Felicity and Flick looked at each other. What was the difference?

"That's exactly what we need for Fanci's party!" announced Danessa. "How do we find it?"

Jayla began squawking excitedly and flapping her flippers.

Preena laughed. "Slow down, slow down," she told her bestie. "There is a story in Frozenwood about a secret ice cream shop with always-frozen ice cream. Jayla's dreamed of going there because they are also supposed to have the best fish ice cream in the whole world."

"Do you think it's a real place?" Patter wondered.

Preena shrugged. "I don't know, but everyone in Frozenwood probably knows the story. Maybe someone there also knows where to look for it."

"We've got to journey there to find out!" exclaimed Felicity.

"Crikey!" Preena laughed. "That would be pawsome!"

Jayla zipped into action, closing the ice cream igloo. Preena took down the sign that said open.

"We're going to see arctic foxes!"

Felicity told Flick.

"And reindeer!" Danessa whispered to Sprint.

A big grin spread across Sprint's face and the bestie tapped an antler with Danessa. He had always wanted to meet a reindeer! This was going to be a real adventure.

"But we have to pack first," Patter realised. "There's so much we need to bring …"

"Don't worry, I've got it all," Felicity said. "Compasses, maps, water bottles … Everybody meet at my house to begin the great expedition to Frozenwood!"

"Hurray!" shouted everyone.

That is, everyone except Flap. He didn't look happy at all.

"What's the matter, little peacock?"

Patter asked him. "Are you worried about being cold?"

Reluctantly, Flap admitted that he was. He loved the heat wave.

"Don't you fret," said Danessa, who'd been listening. "We'll pack mittens and scarves and hats, and you'll be as toasty as … as …"

"As a penguin!" Preena laughed. "Besides, Frozenwood has the best tutti-frutti ice cream. You are going to love it."

Flap smiled at that. And Danessa hoped that no matter what flavour they found, it would stay frozen.

CHAPTER FOUR
TOO COLD FOR COMFORT

Fanci was blowing up pink balloons for
the party in her garden. Pink streamers
hung from the trees and pink roses
were arranged in pink vases on pretty
little pink tables. Fanci's pink flamingo
besties, Swash and Kiba, were practising
poses. Swash slowly lifted a long leg and
tucked it against his belly. Kiba lifted her

beak and stood absolutely still.

Fanci clapped her hands in amazement. "That is just wonderful. If you stand like that when everyone arrives, they will think you are statues and then you can surprise them. We may not have frozen ice cream ... but you two can freeze!"

Swash squawked and Kiba flapped her wings.

"That's it! That's perfect!" exclaimed Fanci. The flamingos struck another set of statue-like poses. "Now all we need to do is work out what we are going to serve instead of ice cream ..."

"No, you don't!" announced Danessa, who had overheard Fanci as she passed by. "I've found never-melting ice cream for your party just like I promised!" Or at least she had a plan to find it. Two plans, really. The last thing she wanted was Fanci to worry about it. Oh deer!

Fanci's face lit up with delight. "Can we taste it? What flavours did you get? Oh, I've got the prettiest pink bowls to serve it in! I hope you got raspberry or strawberry. I'm working with a pink theme."

Danessa nodded, looking around. "It's so pretty! Do you need any help? Sprint and I could blow up balloons for you before we leave, if you want! Or we could hang up more streamers? Or maybe you need some flowers? Sprint and I would be happy to pick some for you. Wouldn't we, Sprint?"

Sprint nodded. He was always ready to lend a helping hoof!

"We're almost done," Fanci told them.

"Where are you going?"

"Preena's taking us to Frozenwood and we are going to bring back ice cream for you in all different flavours," Danessa told her. At least she hoped they were.

Sprint stamped his hoof and Danessa laughed. "Yes, we're getting corn on the cob ice cream for Sprint! And we might even meet a real live reindeer!"

Still, Fanci looked concerned. "I hope you get back in time."

"No more worrying!" Danessa told her. "Let me take care of that. You finish your decorating and let me know if you need anything else before we go!"

She didn't mention that the always-frozen ice cream was only a legend and there was no guarantee that they would find what they were looking for in

Frozenwood. It must be true, Danessa told herself. It had to be. In any case, Bree was working on her invention as well. Somehow there would be ice cream in time for Fanci's party. But maybe she should check on Bree's progress before they left on their journey.

"I have to run," she apologised to Fanci. "But don't you worry one bit. Promise me?"

Fanci nodded. Thank goodness she had such helpful friends.

Swash and Kiba squawked in agreement with a flurry of pink feathers. Danessa and Sprint both jumped in surprise. "Oh! I thought those were Swash and Kiba look-alike statues!"

Fanci clapped her hands, delighted. "We are going to fool everyone. This is going to be the best garden party ever!"

Together, Sprint and Danessa dashed over to Bree's to check on her ice cream invention.

As they approached the cottage, they heard all kinds of noises – clunking, whirring, whizzing and clanking. Big bursts of smoke were coming out the top of the chimney.

"Looks like Bree is busy," Danessa whispered to Sprint. They peeked in through the front door.

A huge contraption was set up on the kitchen table. A long hose ran from the refrigerator to a steel funnel. Liquid dripped into a barrel that was turning around and around. Gears clanked. Mixers churned. Bree was peering into a big bowl that was filling, drop by drop, with something that looked very, very cold.

"Brrr!" Danessa shivered. "Is that making ice cream?"

"Ice cream that can't melt," announced Bree with confidence. "I just need a little more special chillifreeze serum and a drop of vanilla. 'Cause it needs to taste good, too, right?"

"Right!" Danessa agreed.

A cone zipped along a conveyor belt and an automated scoop dipped into the bowl and plopped a frosty dollop on top of it. The ice cream wasn't melting!

Bree and Twist started cheering. Their invention worked! Perfect!

"Maybe we don't even need to go to Frozenwood," Danessa realised. "Can I try it?"

Grinning, Bree handed her friend the cone.

"Mmmmm," said Danessa, beginning to lick. "Mmmph, arrrch, oushhh!" Her tongue was stuck to the ice cream and she could barely talk!

"Quick!" Bree shouted to Twist. "Warm water!"

Bree poured a thin stream of warm water over the cone. Carefully, Danessa pulled off her tongue and rubbed her mouth. Even with warm water running over it, the ice cream wasn't melting. It was like cold metal. Yikes!

"You did it! It's not melting," Danessa told Bree. "But maybe it's a little too cold to eat?"

Bree nodded in agreement. "Back to the drawing board. Less chillifreeze, more rotation during the mixing and maybe a drop more vanilla. How was the flavour?"

"Delicious," Danessa reassured her. "But just a little too chilly! You'll get it right. I know you will. I wish we could stay to help, but we have to hurry. We're leaving for Frozenwood with Preena in just a little bit. She's heard a legend about never-melting ice cream and we are going to find it."

"You mean always-frozen ice cream," said Patter, who had just arrived at the cottage. "Are you packed? I am having so much trouble deciding what to bring! I don't know whether to go with a blue or green or purple colour theme."

"They all sound perfectly you," Danessa told her.

"Ooh, look!" said Patter, noticing the cone. "Ice cream that's not melting." She picked it up to try it.

"Don't lick it!" shouted Danessa and Bree together.

But it was too late. Patter's tongue was stuck to the ice cream.

"Mmmph! Oushhh!" Patter exclaimed.

Twist hopped over with the warm water. Ouch! Patter rubbed her sore tongue. Bree took out a screwdriver and began loosening a bolt on her machine. Danessa blinked, trying to hide her concerns. It was definitely time to head to Frozenwood!

CHAPTER FIVE
READY TO GO (ALMOST)!

Packing was so hard! What should they
bring? How much should they carry?
Felicity had a long list, a giant backpack
and a huge pile of gear for the trip.

"Winter coat and scarf? Check!
Snacks for trip? Check! Flashlight?
Check! And the most important things?"

Felicity looked around the cluttered

room. Ah, there they were. She reached for her compass and her maps. She never left home without them. They needed to travel lightly, but they also didn't want to get lost. At this rate, however, they'd need all Twist's cousins and relatives to carry everything. Oh, and one more thing. "Flick? Flick?" she called. Where was her bestie?

A giant pile of sweaters began to wiggle. Felicity heard a muffled grumble from beneath it. She laughed. "You're under all that stuff?" she asked. "You're supposed to be packed and ready. Let me help you."

Felicity started throwing aside clothes to find the fox and now the room felt messier than ever. Trying to be prepared for every possible emergency had turned her home into an emergency! Where was Flick? She listened carefully and heard the sound of scratching underneath a different pile. Then she saw it – the white tip of a bushy tail.

"Don't move, Flick!" called Felicity. "I'll rescue you!"

Jumpers and scarves flew into the air. What a mess!

Meanwhile, Flap was worried about how to stay warm. The little peacock was busily putting socks and jumpers and hats into an already overstuffed backpack. His long feathers trembled just thinking about Frozenwood. Would his feathers become always-frozen, too?

"It's so hard to know what I'll feel like

wearing ahead of time." Patter sighed. "Like with this blue shirt? I could pair it with either the orange or the purple skirt!"

When Patter wasn't looking, Flap stuffed more mittens into the backpack. But how would he put a mitten on every one of his tail feathers? If only he had down that kept him warm like a snow goose! That was it! Down! He added a puffy vest to the top of the overflowing backpack.

Patter went to pack a carefully folded skirt. But there was no room! What had happened? "Are you bringing everything in the wardrobe, Flap?" she asked her bestie. "Why?"

The peacock hung his head. "Ack, clack, awk," he muttered. "Brrrrr!"

"Oh!" Patter realised Flap didn't want to go to Frozenwood. "Are you afraid it's going to be too cold?"

Flap nodded.

Patter thought for a minute. "How about I help you come up with a plan to stay warm ... like wing warmers!" She showed Flap a special package, designed just for chilly peacocks. "And another thing ... instead of packing those clothes, you can wear them!"

Flap peeped in agreement, but he still looked nervous.

The two emerged from their house a little bit later carrying overstuffed bags and wearing matching outfits. Flap already had on his wing warmers and he was sweating. Ooh! They were wearing far too many clothes for a heat wave in

Wonderwood.

On their way to Flick's, Patter and Flap ran into Preena and Jayla, who were pulling two sleds behind them.

"Hello! Hello!" Preena called out, excited. "Are we ready to go?"

The door to Felicity's cottage opened and out tumbled a giant blob of clothes. A moment later, a flustered Felicity emerged from the middle of the pile. Flick followed, her tail twitching.

"We can't find Flick's backpack!" Felicity worried.

Preena shook her head. "We need to hit the road if we're going to get to Frozenwood before dark."

"Okay, okay," said Felicity, scurrying around. "Lemme take out some of my stuff to make room for Flick's."

Felicity began pulling out all kinds of things from her backpack and tossing them aside. She stuffed in Flick's hat, paints and sketchbook. "We've got a lot of stuff!" She sighed.

"Atta boo!" Jayla was flapping her wings. They had to get going!

Felicity dumped everything in her bag on the ground and began repacking it. Could she make everything fit? She had to. Still, she had the feeling that she was forgetting something, something important. What was it?

With one last worried look around, Felicity threw her backpack over her shoulder. "Ready!" she announced. But she didn't feel ready. If only she'd had more time to pack. But Danessa and Sprint were ready to go. Patter and

Flap were huddled together, looking overdressed and hot.

Just as Preena picked up the reins for one of the sleds, Sage hurried over to the travellers. "I've done it! I've done it!" she shouted. "I've invented never-melting ice cream."

Nobody could believe it! How? But it seemed to be true. In Sage's hand was a scoop of vanilla ice cream and despite the heat, it wasn't melting. Not a drop was dripping down the cone.

"Try it!" Sage urged, handing it to Danessa.

Nervously, her tongue still sore from Bree's freezing-cold invention, Danessa took a lick. It was soft and it wasn't even cold at all. She took a bigger lick and immediately gasped. She carefully tried not to let Sage know she was spitting it out into her hand. "Interesting," she said politely. "Um, it tastes more like mashed potatoes than ice cream ..."

Sage giggled, delighted with her prank. "It is mashed potatoes! And they don't melt!"

Everyone laughed along with her. Still, it was time to go. They had to find never-melting ice cream for real!

CHAPTER SIX
BLOWING HOT AND COLD

Bang! Thunk! Brrrrring! Bree was tinkering with her machine. This time she was going to make it work. She took the hose she had attached to the refrigerator and connected it to the oven. She tightened a screw. She loosened a gear. She poured cream into a big tank.

She added sugar and eggs and vanilla.

"Ca-rumm y taka?" Twist squeaked.

"That's right!" said Bree. "We need carrots and cinnamon! If we are going to make never-melting ice cream, let's make it carrot flavoured!" Bree grated some carrots and added them to the tank. She sprinkled in some cinnamon. This was going to be delicious. She just had to make sure it wasn't too cold again. She flicked a switch on the machine. It began to whir.

The liquid in the tank bubbled and steamed. It smelled yummy. Twist's whiskers twitched in anticipation. She couldn't wait for carrot ice cream.

The working machine made the kitchen so hot. Bree's ears were drooping. But that was okay because this time,

Bree and Twist were making ice cream that was hot and cold at the same time – fried ice cream! Her latest invention was specially designed to make it. After all, if it didn't melt in a fryer, it wouldn't melt at Fanci's garden party. Would it?

Gears were spinning. An ice cube flew across the room. Twist ducked just in time.

"Ears crossed it works," Bree whispered. She removed a bolt from the side of her contraption. That ought to do it.

It was getting hotter and hotter in the kitchen. They were going to need some ice cream to cool off.

"Only a few more minutes!" said Bree.

Chunka, clunk, clunk, thunk! A sizzling circle of fried ice cream spat from the front of the machine. It stopped in front of Bree and Twist. Hot steam rose from it. The crust bubbled.

Twist hopped forward with a fork. She stuck it into the fried ice cream. She lifted it toward her mouth. She took a teeny, tiny bite and she yelped at the top of her lungs. Too hot! Hot as lava! Yikes! Hot!

Bree tried a bite next. Ouch! Twist was right. Much too hot. The ice cream was cold inside, but the outside was burning. Fried ice cream wasn't right.

But what was? Too cold, too hot. How could they make never-melting ice cream that was just right?

"We are not going to give up!" Bree told Twist. "Real inventors never give up. Each time we make a mistake, we are a little closer to getting it right."

Twist nodded. Bree picked up her toolbox. Back to the drawing board!

CHAPTER SEVEN
STOPPING IN THE WOODS

The further north they walked, the cooler it became. Patter was glad she was wearing so many layers now. Felicity and Flick scampered ahead, excited to be on a journey again. Preena and Jayla were telling their friends all about Frozenwood and what to expect.

"There is snow everywhere!" Preena explained. "The whole world is white and everything sparkles like diamonds."

"It sounds beautiful, doesn't it, Sprint?" said Danessa.

Sprint nodded in agreement. Already, the cooler air was making him feel lively. He glanced at Danessa, lowered his head and began to run. Danessa dashed after him, laughing.

Flap grumbled under his breath. It sounded so cold to the peacock. He was already beginning to shiver.

"Will we carry all the ice cream on top of the sledges?" Patter wondered.

Preena shook her head. "See this extra-big lunch box?" She held up an enormous insulated container. "This is what I'll use to carry home the never-melting, everlasting, always-frozen ice cream!"

"Wow!" exclaimed Felicity, coming over to look. "We could take ice cream on all our expeditions!"

Flick's tail swished back and forth happily. That would be wonderful!

"Like when we all visit Junglewood!" Patter suggested. Flap smiled at her. Ice cream in Junglewood sounded perfect.

Jayla made a noise that sounded like the whoosh of waves. She struck a surfer's pose. The penguin wanted to visit the beach – and eat ice cream there!

"Yep, Jayla," agreed Preena. "You could even take ice cream when you're surfing. Cowabunga!"

"Wait, everyone!" called Danessa

breathlessly. She had noticed a little squirrel whose foot was stuck in some tangled grasses. Danessa helped it get free and it squeaked with gratitude before scampering up a pine tree.

"Hey!" said Patter. "Which way do we go?"

The path ahead turned in two different directions through the forest. The trees crowded close and each way looked dark and just a little scary.

"I'll get out my compass and maps!" announced Felicity, taking charge. She rummaged through her backpack. Socks, claw clippers, hats, a tail brush … "Hmmm, I can't find them! What could I have done with them?" She remembered frantically repacking her bag with Flick's things. "Oh," she realised. "I took them out for Flick's stuff and must've forgotten to put them back."

Flap chittered nervously in Patter's ear. "Boo-wa zee?" Were they lost? What if they never were able to get back to somewhere warm again? The peacock's tail opened in a fan.

"We are not lost, Flap," Patter reassured her bestie. "Are we lost?" she asked Preena.

"No, Patter." Preena laughed. "It's been a while, but I'm pretty sure we know the way, right, Jayla?"

Preena pointed to the left confidently. Jayla's wing pointed to the right. Uh-oh.

"Left, right?" said Preena.

Jayla squawked. She wanted to go right. Right?

"This way!" Preena insisted, pulling

her sledge up the path on the left

Jayla went in the opposite direction.

"Both ways can't be right!" worried Felicity. She was still upset. "I really wish we'd found your bag and packed in time, because if we had—"

Flick held up a paw. Stop. Flick rummaged in the backpack and produced her sketch pad and coloured pencils. She began drawing at lightning speed. What was she doing? Was she creating a map? Did she have a plan? Everyone crowded close to watch, including Preena and Jayla.

An instant later, she held up her picture. It showed Felicity looking very, very angry and it made Felicity laugh out loud.

"Making a drawing of my angry

face is not going to help us get to Frozenwood." She smiled. But it had stopped everyone from grumbling and fighting.

"It's very good," Preena noted.

"I have an idea," suggested Patter. "How about we take a break and have a picnic? Then, when we are a little less hungry and angry ..."

"You mean hangry," said Felicity.

"Exactly!" exclaimed Patter. "When we are less hangry, we'll figure out which way to go. Who brought the food?"

"I did!" exclaimed Felicity. But a moment later, her face fell. Uh-oh. She'd unpacked all the snacks along with the compass and the maps. "Noooo! I left the food behind, too."

For the first time, Preena looked

concerned. "We ... we don't have food?"

"Well, you were the one who was in a rush, remember?" noted Patter.

"I know," Preena admitted. "But now I'm hungry and when I get hungry ..."

Jayla made a low cranky noise. "Grrr-rumph."

"I am not cranky," Preena protested crankily.

Patter was beginning to panic. "When I get hungry I get nervous and when I get nervous I have to—"

"We know!" shouted everyone, trying to stop her.

But it was too late. Patter was singing! "La-la-la-la-la!" she warbled off-key.

"Oh deer, oh deer, oh deer! Shhhh!" murmured Danessa. "Shhh! There's no need to be upset. Sprint and I brought snacks. Didn't we, Sprint?"

The deer stamped a hoof and pointed with his antlers at the pack on his back. Danessa began handing out treats.

"Oh, fresh berries! I love fresh berries!" exclaimed Preena.

"And nuts, all different kinds of nuts!" Felicity and Flick were already feeling better. "Thanks, Danessa. Sorry I got cranky."

"Me too," apologised Preena.

"I brought something useful, too," said Patter. She rummaged through her backpack and brought out a silly hat covered in flowers. It was very pretty, but it didn't look very warm.

"Oh!" exclaimed Danessa. The hat looked lovely on Patter.

"Cool!" Felicity complimented her.

"It's pawsome," added Preena. "But will it keep you warm in the freezing cold?"

Patter's eyes widened. "Who said anything about freezing cold?"

"It is called Frozenwood," noted Felicity.

Patter sighed. "Well, just because we are cold doesn't mean we can't be stylish."

"I have an idea," said Danessa. "You can wear that hat on top of another hat! Just like you've done with all your clothes!"

Patter smiled. That was a great idea.

"I've got another idea, too," said Felicity, feeling better after having a bite to eat. "Flap, do you think you could fly above the treetops to see which path we should take? Can you figure out which one heads north?"

Flap's face lit up with pride. Of course he could. He would be happy to help out. The only problem, of course, was flying that high. Could he do it? He could try! He stepped back a bit. He took a deep breath. Slowly, he lurched into the air, flapping his wings as fast as he could. Up, up he flew, higher and higher.

Above the trees, Flap saw the path to the left curve around in the opposite direction. He saw the path to the right go straight ahead and towards snow-capped mountains. That must be the land of Frozenwood. Above the mountains, he saw a single star in the sky. What star was it? The North Star! That was the right direction. It had to be.

Flap slowly came down through the trees and landed in front of the others. He caught his breath and began singing about what he had seen.

"Mountains, snow, the North Star," Patter told the others. "He wants us to go right!"

Jayla smiled at Preena as if to say, I told you so.

"Frozen Mountain is that way!" Patter indicated. She looked up in the sky. She pointed it out to the others.

"Yay!" everyone shouted. They weren't hungry anymore and now they all knew that they were headed in the right direction. That was a relief!

Flap beamed with pride. He didn't feel cold at all.

"Wait!" shouted Danessa to the others

speeding up along the path. She had just
spotted a little mouse who was having
trouble getting into its home. It had
too many seeds stuffed into its cheeks!
"Here," Danessa offered. She carefully
placed a piece of her nutty energy bar
inside its home. Delighted, the mouse
spat out its seeds and scampered into its
hole. "Stay cosy tonight," she told it as
she gently nudged the seeds in behind
the mouse.

She trotted to catch up with her
friends. This really was turning out to be
the best adventure ever.

CHAPTER EIGHT
WITH A GIGGLE
ON TOP

Sage and Caper were very excited about the never-melting ice cream and they wanted to help, too. What better way than finding out what flavours everyone in Wonderwood wanted at Fanci's garden party?

First they stopped to talk to Bren Bear at her shop. Sage pulled out her notebook. "We're helping make some never-melting ice cream for Fanci's big party. Or is it always-frozen ice cream? I can never remember. Anyway, I know you love honey, but are there any other flavours you'd like to try at the party?"

Bren looked thoughtful for a moment. "I love honey so much. I love honey ice cream with honey topping on it. I love honeycomb with honey on top. Don't you?"

"Oh yes," agreed Sage. "I just had some earlier." Her hands were still sticky. "But I want to make sure all the bears like what we create."

"Well, then," Bren said thoughtfully, "salmon ice cream is your best bet."

"Salmon?" Sage wrinkled her nose even while writing down the flavour.

"Isn't it ... fishy?"

"Deliciously fishy!" Bren sighed. "And pink. I happen to know that's one of Fanci's favourite flavours as well."

"We'll have to surprise her, then," said Sage, determined. "Maybe we can have peppermint swirl ice cream, too. That's kind of pink."

"I'm not sure if they would go together ..." Bren said with concern. But Sage and Caper were already out the door. There were lots of Enchantimals to interview.

Who knew there were so many different flavours of ice cream to consider? There were nut flavours like walnut and hazelnut and peanut butter. There were fruit flavours like apple and pear and banana. There were also some

strange flavours like acorn and pine
needle and mushroom!

Caper's nose twitched.

"No mushroom ice cream for us!"
Sage whispered to her bestie.

When they ran into Hixby Hedgehog,
he already knew about the never-melting
ice cream. "Everyone's talking about it!"
he told Sage. "It's just what we need." He
wiped a bead of sweat from his forehead.

"Do you have a favourite flavour?"

"Not really," Hixby admitted. "I
like anything with chocolate – fudge
chocolate, chocolate brownie, white
chocolate and rocky road, of course!"

"Rocky road!" Sage's eyes lit up. That
gave her an idea, a very funny idea. She
whispered something to Caper and her
skunk bestie giggled.

A little later, they stopped to visit Bree and Twist. The kitchen was filled with smoke and a contraption that looked like a cross between a Ferris wheel and a blender was making a high-pitched hissing noise.

Sage looked alarmed. "How's it going?" she asked warily.

Bree's brow wrinkled, concerned. "Well, we still have a few things to work on. We can make so-cold-you-never-want-to-touch-it ice cream and we invented super-sizzling-so-so-hot ice cream, but we're still trying to get one that's just right. Aren't we, Twist?"

Twist thumped her back paws in agreement.

"Well." Sage smiled. "I think Caper and I may have invented the perfect never-melting ice cream all on our own!"

"Really?" Bree couldn't believe it!

Sage held out a cardboard ice cream container. "You wanna try a bite?"

"Yes!" exclaimed Bree and Twist together.

Bree grabbed a spoon, took off the lid … and didn't know what to say. Inside the container were different coloured pebbles. "It's just rocks," she said.

"That's right." Sage giggled. "Rocky road ice cream! Mmmmmmmm! And it doesn't melt!"

"You are too funny, Sage." Bree and Twist laughed together. "Tell you what. If our machine doesn't work and the others don't find what they're looking for in Frozenwood, maybe we can just serve giggles instead!"

CHAPTER NINE
NOT A CLUE

The wind blew across the top of the
mountain. Snowflakes swirled around
the girls and their besties.

"The town's right down the
mountain!" Preena told her friends.

Sprint whinnied with excitement. At
long last, he was going to meet reindeer.

"Frozenwood sure looks frozen," noted
Patter, shivering. "Brrr!"

Flap hovered close. He looked miserable. Even with so many layers and his wing warmers on, he was still so cold.

"Oh deer, I wish I'd thought to bring some hot chocolate!" fretted Danessa. "That would help you feel better"

Flap nodded, trying to be brave.

"We'll be plenty warm when we get back to Wonderwood," said Preena. "We'll want to cool off when we get back there!"

"That's true," agreed Felicity. "C'mon, everyone! Let's go find our never-melting ice cream!"

"You mean always-frozen ice cream," Preena said.

"Same thing, right?" Felicity asked, trying to work out if there was a difference.

Jayla flapped her wings and squawked excitedly. "Za-kaa doo!"

"That's right, Jayla," Preena answered her. "The sledges will be the fastest way to Frozenwood. Hop on, everyone! It's time for the best sleigh ride of your life."

Flick jumped onto the front of one of the sledges and Jayla grabbed the front seat on the other. Even Patter and Flap jumped on board with Sprint and Danessa.

"Look out below, Frozenwood," called Felicity.

"Woo-hoo!" Preena and Jayla said.

"This is wonderful!" Danessa exclaimed.

The sledges went faster and faster and faster. They flew over a bump and both took off into the air. Sprint squealed happily. He felt like a flying reindeer!

The sledges whizzed down the mountain slopes towards the town. The girls and their besties hung on tightly. The snow flew up in their faces and their cheeks were red with the cold. The houses of Frozenwood came closer and closer. The sledges zipped past a surprised moose and skidded to a halt in front of a polar bear who lumbered out of the way.

Sprint stared in amazement. Right in front of him was a real-life reindeer. His antlers were huge! He was really big, a lot bigger than Sprint.

Flick was rummaging through her backpack. There! She found her sketch pad and began drawing.

She wanted to capture everything. The whole town was white and filled with all sorts of animals she'd never seen before. Was that an all-white arctic fox? It was. He was hard to see in the snow.

Flick leapt off the sledge and called out to the arctic fox. She wanted to do his portrait.

The arctic fox looked at her in surprise but happily struck a pose. Flick handed him the picture when she was done and he was very pleased.

Felicity was talking to the snow fox's friend, an Enchantimal girl with a long blond ponytail. "You don't know anything about never-melting ice cream, do you?" she asked.

"That sounds delicious, but no, I've never heard of it. I wish we had never-gets-cold chocolate, too!"

Sprint and Danessa were introducing themselves to the reindeer. "Are you very cold living up here so far north?" Danessa asked. "I've been thinking that maybe we should organise a jumper-knitting campaign in Wonderwood to bring you warmer winter wear."

Sprint stamped his hoof to get Danessa's attention.

"Oh," remembered Danessa, "have you heard of never-melting ice cream?"

The reindeer shook his head. He hadn't.

Felicity approached a group of girls skating on a frozen pond. She asked every one of them if they had heard of never-melting ice cream, but no one had. She talked to a walrus who was working on an ice sculpture, but he shook his long tusks no.

"I'm worried," Danessa told Preena. "It sounds like the legend might be just that."

But Preena was determined. "Everyone keeps asking about never-melting ice cream. We need to ask about ice cream that's always-frozen."

"Right!" said all the girls, listening. Did it really make a difference?

Together they visited all the shops in Frozenwood. They went to the penguin café and the seal hardware shop. They talked to polar bears and puffins and made sure to ask about always-frozen ice cream. But no one knew anything about it.

Preena felt terrible. "Sorry," she apologised to the others. "It looks like only Jayla and I know the legend of the always-frozen ice cream … and maybe there is no such thing after all."

"That's all right," answered Patter, her teeth chattering with the cold. "This is still fu-fu-fun."

Felicity nodded. She had picked up lots of new postcards and posters of Frozenwood for her collection. "Maybe we should head home and plan things a bit better for next time. There's got to be other places to look. We can have another adventure looking for never-melting – I mean, always-frozen – ice cream."

"At least we aren't hot anymore, right?" Danessa said, trying to look on the bright side.

Everyone had to agree. It was cold in Frozenwood. Really cold. The wind blew off the mountain and made them shiver.

Jayla squinted and stared at the mountain. She tugged on Preena's arm. She chirped and peeped.

"Hang on, Jayla," said Preena. "What other places do you think we should look?" she asked Felicity.

Felicity shrugged. "Some place we don't know about yet."

Jayla was stamping her feet and waving her wings.

"One sec, Jayla." Preena sighed.

Frustrated, Jayla stomped off, pulling her sledge behind her.

"Jayla?" Preena called after her. "Where are you going?"

"What is Jayla doing?" wondered Felicity.

Jayla had stomped up a small hill with

her sledge and was now standing on it as if it were a snowboard. The penguin spread her wings wide like a surfer and zoomed down the hill, going faster and faster. She hit a bump and flew into the air on the sledge, holding it with her wings. She turned a circle and landed perfectly – right on the top of a billboard.

"What are you …?" began Preena. Her mouth hung open. Her eyes widened.

"It's a picture of a snowy mountain?" said Patter, confused.

"Is that important?" Felicity asked.

"Of course it is!" exclaimed Preena. "Oh, Jayla, you are brilliant!"

"What? What?" asked the girls and their besties all at once.

Preena grinned. "See that mountain? What does it look like?"

All the girls stared at the picture on the billboard. It showed a triangular mountain with a round dollop of white snow at the top. It did look like something familiar, but what?

"An ice cream cone!" realised Danessa.

"An ice cream cone that's always frozen," explained Preena. "That's Frozen Mountain! That must be the home of the always-frozen, never-melting ice cream! Not only are you the best snowboarder, Jayla, you are the best detective, too!"

On top of the billboard, Jayla took a bow.

CHAPTER TEN
BRAND-NEW FLAVOURS

Bree's newest contraption was clanking and clunking in her kitchen. Twist was holding a hammer in one paw and a bottle of sticky tree sap in another and she had a carrot between her ears.

"Ready to grate more carrot, Twist?" asked Bree, trying not to yawn.

The bunny nodded, but she was tired,

too. Still, if they were going to invent ice cream that wasn't too cold, wasn't too hot and never melted, it had better taste like carrot cake. Right? Twist got to work.

Bree adjusted the temperature on the machine. She poured a grey liquid into a funnel. The invention rumbled and roared.

"Peee-yew!" said Sage, coming into the kitchen.

Caper's nose wrinkled. She took out a bottle of perfume and began spraying it around the room.

"Is it supposed to smell like that?" asked Sage curiously.

"I'm focusing on the melting right now," Bree answered. But Sage was right, there was a terrible smell coming from the inside of the machine.

"What if I told you that Caper and I just invented ice cream that doesn't melt?" Sage giggled.

"I wouldn't believe you." Bree laughed.

"You should! Let me show it to you!" Sage said confidently.

Bree and Twist crowded around. "Where is it?" asked Bree.

Sage held up a fist. "Here! Try my newest flavour!"

Bree was confused.

Sage giggled. "It's invisible ice cream!" She pretended to take a lick from an ice cream cone. "Mmmmm, yummy. You can almost taste it if you shut your eyes. And it doesn't melt!"

Bree laughed. "That's true! But there's only one problem."

"What?" asked
Sage.

"It doesn't cool
you off and it's not
going to work for
Fanci's party ..."

"Oh," said Sage.
"I'm coming up with lots of jokes and
pranks. No one will even notice that
there's no ice cream!"

A bowl flipped over on a conveyer
belt and wobbled along underneath the
funnel. It emerged with a round pale-
green scoop inside it.

Sage peered into the bowl. "Is that a
joke?"

"That's ice cream that doesn't melt,"
Bree explained. "You want to try a bite?"

Sage gulped. The ice cream did not

smell nice. "What flavour is it?"

"Carrot cake," answered Bree.
"I think."

"You think?"

"Well," Bree said, "I had to add a lot of other things to the mix to make sure it wouldn't melt."

Sage stuck a spoon into the pale-green goop in the bowl. She tried to scoop a tiny bite, but she couldn't. The spoon was stuck to the ice cream.

"What's going on?" Sage asked. "Is this a prank?"

Twist shook her head. "Ma a-ta-ta …"

Bree agreed with what her bestie was saying. "You're right. Too much sap."

"Ewww! Sap!" Sage dropped the bowl and the spoon. They clattered to the floor.

Bree shrugged. "I made sure it was edible! And it doesn't melt. Look!"

It was true. The scoop was stuck to the bowl. The spoon was stuck to the goop. But it was not a refreshing treat for a garden party.

"We better work on some more jokes," Sage whispered to Caper.

"Back to the drawing board." Bree sighed to Twist. "We just need to invent ice cream that's not too cold, not too hot …"

"And not too weird," finished Sage. "I wonder how the team in Frozenwood is doing. I wonder if they ever found always-frozen ice cream …"

Everyone in the kitchen was hoping that their friends had.

CHAPTER ELEVEN

UP, UP AND AWAY!

"Which one is Frozen Mountain?" asked
Felicity, looking at the snow-covered
peaks in the distance.

"That one!" said Preena, pointing at
the biggest. Its summit was hidden in the
clouds.

Patter gulped. "How do we climb all
the way up that?" Flap was clinging to

her arm nervously. That was a lot higher than he had ever flown.

Jayla was pointing at the billboard with her wing.

"Don't worry!" Preena laughed. "There's a funicular to get to the top! That's what the advertisement is for. We just buy a ticket, hop in and it whisks us up, up, up into the sky!"

"What's a funicular?" asked Felicity, peering at the picture on the billboard. "It looks like a train that goes straight up."

"That's exactly what it is!" Preena answered.

"Chrip prr felah!" Jayla peeped and chirped excitedly, explaining that for a penguin it was the closest to flying she had ever come.

"Does it go really fast?" Patter asked nervously.

"So fast!" Preena told her, not realising her friend was already frightened by the funicular.

"I know," said Patter with a nervous gulp. "I'll sing. That helps when I feel scared. La-la-la-la-LA!"

"And I'll hold your hand," promised Danessa. She couldn't wait to ride on the funicular but she could understand how scary it might feel for Patter and Flap.

"Do you need another scarf?" Danessa asked Flap.

He shook his head. He couldn't tell if he was shivering from the cold or because he was nervous.

"C'mon, everybody!" Preena called from the sledges. "We've got to hurry.

Fanci's party is tomorrow."

The sledges raced across the frozen roads and reached the funicular in no time. Felicity and Flick grabbed window seats but Patter and Flap covered their eyes. It was worse than being on the highest roller coaster and they hated amusement park rides. Peacocks liked to stay close to the ground, even when they were flying.

"Hold my hand," Danessa reminded her.

But Patter was already thinking about how fast they must be moving. "La-la-la-la-LA," she sang, louder and louder.

The others covered their ears, trying not to listen to her off-key singing.

"LA-LA-LA-LA-LA!"

The faster the funicular went, the louder Patter sang.

Off in the distance, Felicity heard the rumble of thunder. "Can it thunder and snow at the same time?" she wondered out loud.

"We're almost at the top," Preena told everyone.

The rumbling grew louder and louder. Patter's singing became a high-pitched screech. "Leeeeeeeeeeee-leeeeeeeeeeeeeeeeee-leeeeeeeeeeeeeeeeee!"

"What is that noise?" asked Danessa. "Not Patter. But that other noise, the one that sounds like surf at the ocean about to crash on the beach …"

Preena stood up, alarmed. "Grab hands, everyone!"

"What? Why?"

"Avalanche!" Preena shouted, just before a wall of snow hit the funicular.

The funicular screeched to a halt. Patter's singing had started an avalanche! A giant wave of snow washed over their car, roaring past them. When they looked out the windows, all they could see was white.

"Follow me, everyone!" said Preena. "We're going to tunnel our way out."

"I can help!" said Felicity. "Flick and I are great at burrowing!"

Moments later, the girls and their besties popped out through the snow. The sun sparkled in the blue sky and a huge patch of snow was gone from the top of the mountain, revealing a big purple and green building.

"What's that big house?" Felicity

wondered. "What's it doing at the top of Frozen Mountain?"

Jayla started jumping up and down excitedly. Preena grinned. "The legend is true!"

"What? What?" asked the girls.

Preena pointed at the building. "That is the Always-Frozen, Never-Ending Ice Cream Emporium that I've always heard about! The snow has hidden it all this time. But it's always been right here! Without your singing, Patter, we never would have found it. You saved the day!"

Patter was stunned. "Really?"

Danessa shook some snow from her antlers. "Oh wow!" she exclaimed. "I can hardly believe it. But now we can keep our promise to Fanci!" She and Sprint began doing their bestie ritual, touching their antlers and tapping their hooves.

"So I guess my singing isn't so bad after all," said Patter.

The girls and their besties didn't know what to say.

"Well," replied Danessa carefully, "maybe no more singing … for now. I think one avalanche is all that we need for today."

"Absolutely," agreed Felicity and Preena.

"Now let's go get some ice cream," Danessa announced.

"Brrrrrr!" muttered Patter. "I hope they also serve always-warm hot chocolate!"

CHAPTER TWELVE
TURNING LEMONS INTO LEMONADE

Bree's kitchen was a mess. The sink was loaded with dirty pots and pans and goop-covered spoons. The toolbox was open and there were hammers, screwdrivers and wrenches all over the counters. The remains of three different machines lay in pieces on the floor. Bree and Twist were flipping through the pages of a science manual. They looked very tired.

Bree sighed. "Twist, I won't be defeated, but I don't know what we should do next. All our inventions have been total lemons."

Twist thumped her feet, wiggled her whiskers, and squeaked, "Squee la-boo!"

Bree laughed. "All right then, let's make lemonade! At least that will cool us off. But let's do it the old-fashioned way."

Together they squeezed lemons into a jug, then added ice, water and a little touch of sugar. "Ah!" Bree smiled, tasting it. "Maybe we should just tell Fanci to serve this instead? We could invent a special lemonade machine, right? It would squeeze the lemons, fill the glass with ice and you could program it for different amounts of sugar. How hard would that be?"

Twist grinned. That sounded a lot easier than never-melting ice cream.

They were just beginning to attach some tubing to the refrigerator's ice machine when Sage and Caper popped in.

"What kind of never-melting ice cream do you have for us this time?" asked Bree.

Sage plonked down onto a chair. "All my jokes have melted!"

Caper stretched out beside her, panting. It was so hot.

"Maybe we need to go on a journey to look for always-frozen pranks. What do you say, Caper?"

But the skunk bestie was too tired even to laugh.

"Would you like a glass of lemonade?" offered Bree.

"Yes!" answered Sage and Caper.

But by the time Bree carried it across the room, the ice in the glass had melted.

"Everything's melting," noted Sage. "Even my hair."

"I'm dreaming about ice cream," admitted Bree. "Cold, refreshing, delicious ice cream!"

"Coffee, chocolate, mocha and mint." Sage sighed.

"Ripple, brickle, caramel swirl," riffed Bree.

"Blueberry, butterscotch and butter pecan," added Sage. This was beginning to be fun. She picked up a pan and a metal spoon and began banging out a drumbeat.

"Peanut butter, brownie and chocolate chip!" Bree chanted.

"Sundaes, splits and soft-serve cones!" Now Sage was singing. Caper started humming along.

Bree joined in. "Sherbets, sorbets and syrup-covered ice!"

Caper picked up some wooden spoons and was adding to the beat. Twist wasn't looking tired anymore. She began to wiggle her tail and dance.

Sage paused, catching her breath. "I just realised something else that doesn't melt."

"What?" asked Bree.

"Our voices! Let's write an ice cream song! That won't melt and just thinking about ice cream will cool off everyone."

"It will!" Bree agreed.

"We may not be able to make it or find it or eat it, but we can sing about it!"

The girls decided to clean Bree's kitchen first and then head over to Sage's. She had lots of instruments, including a drum set and a keyboard. On their way through the village, they kept running into friends who were excited about Fanci's garden party. They let them know that they had a secret plan for the party!

"You can count on the ice cream dream team," Bree promised. "See you tomorrow at the party!" She waved goodbye to their friends.

"The ice cream dream team!" whispered Sage excitedly. "I like that.

Maybe we can work it into the song!"

"How do we write lyrics?" wondered Bree when they reached Sage's house.

Sage smiled as she set up her drum kit. "The same way you cook up something new – a little bit of this, a little bit of that and a lot of inspiration and imagination."

Bree and Twist sat side by side at the keyboard and tried out different chords. Slowly, they began to find a tune and hum along.

Listening to them, Sage and Caper started adding a beat with the drums. "Pick a flavour," Sage improvised.

"Do yourself a favour! Pick yourself a flavour!" rhymed Bree.

The girls laughed as they tossed lines back and forth. They jotted down ones they liked in a notebook and played around with different tunes. They barely noticed the heat anymore as they were too busy having fun.

"What rhymes with swirl?" Bree wondered.

Caper immediately had an answer for her.

"Squirrel! That's right. I think I can make that work!" Bree clapped her hands, delighted.

"Ooooh! I've got another line," announced Sage a moment later. "Summer turns to winter with an ice cream cone!"

"It sure does,"

agreed Bree. "Just thinking about ice cream makes me forget the heat!"

"Is it hot? I hadn't noticed." Sage laughed.

"I think we've got it," said Bree at last.

"Let's try out the whole thing!" Sage agreed. "And a one and a two ..."

"Do yourself a favour! Pick yourself a flavour!

One scoop, two scoop, it's time to cool down!

Coffee, chocolate, mocha and mint,

Vanilla, caramel and chocolate chip!

Do yourself a favour! Pick yourself a flavour!

One scoop, two scoop, it's time to cool down!

Ripple, brickle and peanut-butter swirl,

Blueberry, raspberry and nuts for the squirrels!

Do yourself a favour! Pick yourself a flavour!

One scoop, two scoop, it's time to cool down!

Snowflakes, blizzard, chill us to the bone.

Summer turns to winter with an ice cream cone.

Do yourself a favour! Pick yourself a flavour!

One scoop, two scoop, it's time to cool down!"

CHAPTER THIRTEEN
EVERYTHING UNDER THE SUN

The Always-Frozen, Never-Ending Ice
Cream Emporium was a magical place,
painted in all kinds of bright, cheerful
colours. Brass chairs were arranged
around small, round tables. A polished
wood counter wrapped around the
middle of the room and behind it were
hundreds of different flavours of ice
cream.

Winsley, an Enchantimal girl with a wolf bestie at her side, greeted them as they came in. "Welcome! 'If you've imagined it, we've made it!' That's our motto!"

"Am I dreaming?" Preena asked.

Felicity looked around, pawstruck. "It's really happening."

Even Flap was thrilled. He pointed his wings at the different flavours. There was hot-chocolate-flavoured ice cream. He was jumping up and down!

Danessa couldn't believe it. "There's carrot cake for Bree! And pistachio and green tea for you and me, Sprint!"

"Chocolate, dark chocolate, white chocolate, chocolate chip, triple fudge, dark chocolate with chocolate swirls, moose tracks ..." read Felicity. "How can

I choose?"

Flick began barking excitedly.

"Me too!" Felicity laughed, agreeing
with her bestie. "I want one of each!
Let's try every flavour. Do you give out
samples?"

"Of course we do!" said Winsley.
"What would you like to try?"

The girls and their besties clustered
close, trying to decide. Patter and Flap
tried a taste of tutti-frutti.

"That ice cream is just as good as
yours, Preena! And your ice cream
is the best I've ever had!" exclaimed
Patter. "I'm surprised everyone from
Frozenwood isn't here!"

Winsley shook her head. "We don't get
a lot of business. Most people don't even
know we're here. When you live in a cold

place, you like warm things – cookies fresh out of the oven, hot soup and steaming hot chocolate … not ice cream."

"That's why I opened my igloo truck in Wonderwood," explained Preena. "How many flavours can we fit in my insulated lunch box, I wonder?"

"This ice cream is always-frozen, right?" Danessa asked.

" 'On Frozen Mountain, the ice cream is always-frozen!' " Winsley told her. "That's another one of our mottos!"

"Let's get a tub of every flavour to bring back with us," Preena suggested. "It's impossible to choose. I wish I knew how to make always-frozen ice cream."

"It's not hard. I'd be happy to give you the recipe," Winsley offered.

"Really?"

Jayla was jumping up and down.

"Can you imagine?" Preena turned to the others. "We could have always-frozen ice cream all the time! Everyone is going to be so happy!"

Winsley scooped tubs of ice cream and handed them to Preena, who put them in her special bag.

"I cannot wait to try the green tea," Danessa whispered to Sprint.

Sprint nodded in agreement.

When they were finally finished, Winsley handed a small recipe book to Preena. "It's been in my family a long time," she told her. "Just tell your friends to come and visit me anytime."

"We will," promised Danessa. "You are going to have lots and lots of visitors from Wonderwood."

"Wonderwood?" Winsley was amazed. "Wow! Is it warmer there?"

"A lot warmer," Patter told her.

"But not as sparkly," Danessa added. "It's so pretty here."

"If you're from Wonderwood, you can catch the next raft that leaves Icy Babbling Brook."

"Babbling Brook is here?" Felicity was surprised.

"It starts here on Frozen Mountain," said Winsley with pride. "But you'd better hurry. The raft only goes to Wonderwood once a day and it leaves Icy Babbling Brook in five minutes."

A bell began ringing in the distance. Quickly, Preena closed her special lunch box and the girls gathered up their things.

"Can I have just one more taste of tutti-frutti?" Patter asked Winsley, but the wolf was already handing out cones to all the girls.

"These are gifts from me," said Winsley. "It's been great to have you here. Come again soon. 'In the Always-Frozen, Never-Ending Ice Cream Emporium, our smiles are never-ending, too!' That's another one of our mottos!"

"I'm going to help you get the word out about this place," Danessa told her. "Everyone should know what a wonderful job you are doing. You deserve lots of customers. You really do! I promise to give you a little help when I get back. Don't you worry! Leave that to me."

"Hurry!" Preena called from the door. It was time to board the express raft to

Wonderwood.

The girls and their besties ran as fast as they could down a walkway that led to Icy Babbling Brook. The raft looked like a giant boat with ice skates.

"What a great adventure this has been." Felicity sighed happily. She settled down on the raft. Flick cuddled close to her.

In an instant, the raft was off, slipping and sliding down Icy Babbling Brook at high speed.

"Wheeee!" squealed Preena and Jayla.

"Ahhhhhhhh!" shouted Danessa and Sprint, clutching each other.

"I am not going to sing I am not going to sing I am not going to sing," Patter told herself. Flap shut his eyes as tightly as he could.

The raft hurtled down the mountain, whizzed through the village of Frozenwood and finally began to slow down when it entered the wide waters of the forest. Flap opened his eyes and saw the trees all around them on either side. Patter began to feel like she could breathe again.

Preena opened the little book Winsley had given her. She couldn't wait to get home and make always-frozen ice cream. She studied the recipes. But something was strange. They looked exactly like the ice cream she always made. Was there a special machine she needed? Or a missing ingredient? She'd have to study the book more carefully when she got home. Now, she was tired. She snuggled up to Jayla.

Lulled by the lapping of water against the side of the raft, the girls and their besties began to fall asleep one by one. The sun set. The stars came out.

Sleepily, Flick pointed up to the sky with her paw.

"Ah, the North Star again." Felicity yawned. "We had a great adventure after all, even without a map and compass." She wrapped her tail around Flick's and shut her eyes.

All the girls and their besties were lost in dreams. During the night, a cool wind began to blow and they huddled up together.

CHAPTER FOURTEEN
A WARM REUNION

The raft glided along the gentle waters
of Babbling Brook to Wonderwood. The
sun dappled through the trees. The girls
and their besties stretched and yawned,
awakening. They had shed their coats
and their mittens. But Flap didn't want
to take off his wing warmers yet. He was
still a little cold.

The girls kept on their jumpers, too. There was a chill in the air.

"It's almost as if we've brought the cold back with us," said Patter, shivering a little.

"I wish." Preena sighed. It had been nice to visit her home again. "Still, I'm so excited to be bringing back always-frozen ice cream."

"Here we are!" called out Felicity.

The raft bumped against a wooden dock and Felicity jumped out, lending a hand to help the others.

"Look!" said Danessa, pointing to one of the maple trees. "Since we've been gone, some of the leaves have begun to turn red and gold."

Felicity helped Preena carry the big container with all the different flavours of always-frozen ice cream. They had just enough time to stop by Sage's and change their clothes before the party.

As they got closer to the cottage, they heard a steady beat of drums and a foot-tapping tune.

"I don't know that song," said Danessa. "But I like it."

"Do yourself a favour! Pick yourself a flavour!

One scoop, two scoop, it's time to cool down!"

"Hey, that's catchy!" Felicity said as they walked into Sage's.

The girls put down their instruments when they saw their friends. "Did you find it? Is the legend true?"

"It is!" said Preena. "Always-frozen ice cream right here!" She tapped the giant suitcase.

"And it's the best ice cream you've ever had!" Patter added. "Or rather, it's the best always-frozen ice cream. Preena's tastes just as good when it doesn't melt."

Preena smiled at her gratefully, but her comment made her wonder again about those recipes. They were just the same as hers. What was the missing ingredient that kept the ice cream always frozen?

"Well, we wrote an ice cream song!" Bree told everyone.

"We heard a little bit of it," said Felicity. "It sounds great."

"Did you invent a machine to make never-melting ice cream?" Danessa asked Bree.

"Almost," she answered. "But the only one that was even close had too much sap …"

"But," she added, "Sage made an absolutely delicious rocky road ice cream. Sage, you'll have to give everyone a taste!"

"At the party!" Sage giggled. "I've got it all ready."

The girls hurried to change out of their travel clothes into their best party attire. Flick showed Caper and Twist some of the pictures she had drawn on the trip. The animals looked in amazement at the giant snow-covered mountains. Brrr! They looked cold!

A gust of wind blew through the trees.

Wonderwood wasn't feeling so hot anymore. At all. The air was chilly.

CHAPTER FIFTEEN
A BREATH OF FRESH AIR

"Look at those lawn ornaments!" marvelled Preena, seeing the flamingo statues in the garden.

"Squawk!"

All the girls jumped!

"Those aren't statues!" Fanci laughed. "Those are my besties! But I'm glad you are all here. Can you help me move my party inside? It's too cold for a garden party! I've lit a fire in the fireplace!"

Patter squawked happily at the thought of a fire.

As fast as they could, the girls and their besties carried tables and chairs into Fanci's living room. They unfurled the streamers from the trees and grabbed handfuls of pink balloons. Carefully, they carried in trays of tea party sandwiches and jugs of lemonade and put them on the counter. Wind blew across the lawn. Golden leaves fell from the trees. Squirrels scurried here and there collecting nuts.

"Put on a party hat!" urged Fanci. "That will help you warm up!" She handed out little pink party hats to everyone. They were adorable but not very practical. A fire crackled in the fireplace. The girls and their besties crowded around it, warming their hands and paws.

"Whew!" Felicity exclaimed. "We got back from Frozenwood just in time! Imagine how cold it's gotten there!"

"You really went to Frozenwood?" Fanci was stunned.

"To get always-frozen ice cream for your party!" Danessa told her.

"And we've got every flavour you could ever imagine," added Patter. "Even honey with salmon."

All the girls and the animals crowded close as Preena produced her special ice cream box.

"May I have a drumroll, please!" she

called to Sage, who had been setting up her instruments.

"You got it!" Sage answered. She and Caper began a suspense-filled tremor.

"Ta-da!" announced Preena, opening the lid. The wind howled outside, adding to the excitement.

But inside the case was not always-frozen ice cream. Inside the case was a messy swirl of perfectly melted ice cream soup.

"But how?" wondered Preena. "How could always-frozen ice cream melt?"

Patter placed a comforting hand on her shoulder. "Maybe always-frozen, never-melting ice cream only exists when you're in Frozenwood."

"Maybe it's always-frozen on Frozen Mountain but not anywhere else," realised Danessa.

"Maybe that's why the recipes are exactly the same as mine!" exclaimed Preena. "Because they are!"

"I guess always-frozen ice cream and never-melting ice cream really are two different things," Felicity whispered to Flick.

Danessa turned to Fanci. She felt terrible. "We've ruined your party. We promised we would bring you ice cream and we failed."

Bree felt bad, too. If only one of her inventions had worked.

"Step right up for a cone of invisible ice cream!" announced Sage, holding a pretend cone in her hand. "We've got every flavour and it never melts." She took an imaginary taste. "It's yummy!"

Everyone laughed, especially Fanci. "You know," she said, "look at how everyone's shivering. I don't think I want ice cream right now anyway. I don't think anyone does!"

Fanci was right. The girls had goose bumps on their arms.

"Brrrr," said Patter. "I am cooler."

Jayla started jumping up and down, flapping her wings and chirping. She had an idea!

"That's it!" agreed Preena. "We'll be right back, everyone!" They closed the ice cream case, grabbed it and rushed out.

What was she going to do?

"While we're waiting, let's warm up and dance!" said Sage, beating her drums.

Bree took her place on the keyboards and began playing their ice cream song. Soon everyone was singing along and dancing.

"Coffee, chocolate, mocha and mint,

Vanilla, caramel and chocolate chip!

Do yourself a favour! Pick yourself a flavour!

One scoop, two scoop, it's time to cool down!"

The ringing of a bell interrupted their singing. It was Preena and Jayla with their igloo ice cream truck. They had driven right up to Fanci's front door. As the girls and their besties stepped outside, the sun emerged from behind the clouds. But the air was so much cooler now. The heat wave was over.

Sprint shook his antlers in the

direction of trees turned golden and red.

"I think you are right, Sprint," said Danessa to her bestie. "I think while we were away, autumn arrived!"

"Hooray!" shouted everyone.

Preena and Jayla looked out from the window of the ice cream truck. "Get your always yummy, refreshing but not frozen … smoothies! All-new flavours from Frozenwood! 'When you don't need to cool down but you do want a yummy treat.' I think that's our motto!"

Bren Bear rushed over to be first in line. "Honey with salmon for me!" she ordered.

"Coming right up!" answered Preena.

"Chocolate swirl with chocolate!" Hixby ordered.

Fanci couldn't have been happier.

"Oooh! Smoothies! How perfect for a party! I love smoothies! That's the best idea ever! Not too cold and not too warm. They are just right!"

Not only was Danessa relieved, but she had another great idea. "We need to go back to Frozenwood," she told Sprint. "This will save Winsley's emporium. She needs to offer smoothies as well as ice cream! When people are cold, they'll like smoothies better."

"Great idea!" said Felicity, who'd overheard her.

"But right now I have an even better idea," volunteered Sage. "Leaf piles!"

She'd raked all the fallen leaves into a huge pile and she and Caper dived in! Everyone else followed, laughing.

"Oh!" Fanci sighed happily.

"Leaf piles, smoothies, laughter, songs and good friends. This is the best party ever!"

THE END

DISCOVER MORE
ENCHANTIMALS BOOKS!